BAMBOOZLED

For my best friend,
mentor, and wife, Rhonda. DL

Legge, David, 1963–.

    Bamboozled.

    ISBN 0 86896 987 7 (pbk.).

    I. Title.

A823.3

First published in hardback in 1994 by Ashton Scholastic Pty Limited.

This edition published in 1996 by Scholastic Australia Pty Limited
ACN 000 614 577, PO Box 579, Gosford 2250. Also in Sydney, Brisbane,
Melbourne, Adelaide, Perth and Auckland NZ.

Packaged for Ashton Scholastic by Donna Rawlins.

This book was typeset in Century Old Style.

The illustrations for this book were painted with watercolours.

Typeset by Asset Typesetting Pty Ltd, Sydney.

Printed in Hong Kong.

9 8 7 6 5 4 3 2 1   6 7 8 9 / 9

BAMBOOZLED

DAVID LEGGE

SCHOLASTIC
SYDNEY AUCKLAND NEW YORK TORONTO LONDON

I love my grandad.
I visit him every week.
And every week, things are
the same.
But *last* week when I arrived,
something seemed odd.

We sat down, as usual, and
chatted for a while.
Then Grandad poured the tea
and we ate fresh cakes he'd
baked that morning.

We played cards,

and, as always, he won.

We went through his old
photo albums and I listened
as he told stories about
The Good Old Days.

I helped him with the
housework, but all the while,
something bothered me.

We worked in the garden, and I planted bulbs in the flower bed.

I pushed the wheelbarrow while Grandad pruned the roses. And still, something seemed strange. It niggled and niggled at the back of my mind.

'You *are* quiet today,' Grandad said as he fed the cat.

'I know,' I said. 'I can't make it out. There's something I can't put my finger on. Something, today, seems odd.'

'Well — I've redecorated the hallway.'

No, I thought, it wasn't that.

'I've bought two new fish.'

No, it wasn't that either.

Then, just as we were saying our goodbyes on the doorstep, it suddenly struck me.

'Grandad!' I said. '*That's* what it is.

You're wearing odd socks!'

Silly Grandad.
We *did* laugh.